MW01042372

DISCARDED

The Kingdom of Grape

RAIMO STRANGIS

ISBN: 9781461036760

For Nelleah and Alyssa

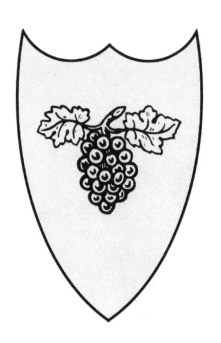

I

This is the story of the brave but careless Donnie Drake. Donnie is a common man living in a rich and prosperous kingdom, the Kingdom of Grape. He was born and raised in Grape but didn't know his parents for long. At the age of two, Donnie tragically lost his parents during a time of war. After their passing, Donnie was left to be raised by the town's caretakers.

Grape is a kingdom divided in wealth and in stature. There are those who have and those who pick. Donnie's parents were grape pickers and worked hard every day so Donnie could one day have a better life. Grape pickers are treated poorly and looked down upon by the upper class. Because of this, there was a great civil war. The common people banded together to revolt against the upper class. The fight was led by Donnie's father, Grenache Drake. Though they fought honorably, they were no match for the army of the kingdom. Commanded by General Malbec Red, the army used deceitful tactics to win the war, which were unbeknown to the king.

Donnie was rescued and brought to the Riesling Orphanage to be raised by the angels that worked there. The orphanage was a beautiful place. It was a small but well-built hut which divided the Chardonnay and Merlot Grape fields. Led by Lady Rose, the caregivers had no prejudice and treated the children as if they were their own. There, Donnie would learn to love and care for others, and to respect the lands that surround them.

As Donnie grew, the ladies began to see that Donnie was no ordinary child. Every time King Earl Grape visited, Lady Rose would mention they had a child of great promise.

Sixteen years later, at the age of eighteen, with the recommendation of Lady Rose, Donnie was approved by the king to become the kingdom's messenger. He cherishes that moment as one of the best days in his life.

Donnie moved to a place of his own not too far from the orphanage. He lives a simple life, with just a guitar to strum and dreams of one day having a family of his own. The sounds of his music echo throughout the kingdom at starlight.

Every morning Donnie collects the letters left at his doorstep and delivers them throughout the town on horseback. Pinot is more than just a horse, he is also Donnie's most trusted companion. Pinot is smaller than most horses, pure white, and sports an impressive golden mane.

Donnie and Pinot love their job. It allows them to see all the town's beauty: its soft green hills, the cobblestone roads, and the endless grapevines connecting the very soul of the kingdom. Donnie is content and accepts his common place in the kingdom. But, little did he know, that is all about to change.

Donnie's route always begins with a visit to Lady Gates. One of the most respected and imperial residents of Grape, Lady Gates has a very important responsibility. She is the keeper of the most precious treasure of all, the ancient seeds of Grape. These seeds date back hundreds of years cultivated by the original ancestors of Grape. However, Donnie has a different view of the lady. Her arrogance is a constant reminder of the division in Grape.

"Hello, here are your messages sent with luck, Lady Gates," Donnie says politely.

"Give them here, boy, and clean yourself up. Those who present like an animal are destined to become one." she says loudly, so her aristocratic peers can hear. As usual, Donnie lowers his head and continues his route.

In contrast, the finest moment in Donnie's day is when his deliveries take him to Castle Grape, home of the great King Earl Grape. The castle is a marvel, with giant stone walls soaring to the sky, and endless towers cloaked with the flags and crests of the kingdom. Grapevines grow like ivy, covering the front gates. The bricks are colored with the maroon pigment of the ancient grapes. But, it's not just the king that Donnie is eager to see; it's the princess that makes his heart sing, Princess Jane Grape.

Whenever he lays eyes on her, warmth and adoration overcome him. No one else has ever made him feel this way. Donnie adores how she treats the people of Grape. On her daily rides, Jane meets with everyone, no matter their stature, and offers an ear and heart to anyone in need. Even though they have never met, Donnie knows she is his one true love.

Donnie approaches the castle, but before he can even speak the guard shouts,

"Leave your messages and go, boy!"

"Oh, pardon, please deliver these letters to the king, with luck."

Donnie stretches his neck, trying desperately to catch a glimpse of the princess. If only he could find the courage to express his love for her. He loves everything about her, her wavy brown hair, her light green eyes, and her irresistible beauty. Yet, Donnie knows she could never love a common man like him, for she is set to marry a feared and frightening man named Duke the Red.

A chill comes over Donnie as he turns to leave the castle gates. He feels the earth rumble beneath him as a monster of a man approaches on a giant black horse. It's Duke the Red. The duke seems eight feet tall and made of solid stone. He is dressed in heavy metal armor, covered with badges of honor.

Some say he carries a sword so sharp it can slice a tree trunk with one swift strike.

The duke's father, General Malbec Red, led the army to victory during the historic civil battle. Once the war was over, General Malbec and King Earl formed a strong bond and made an oath that their children would marry one day. Thus, King Earl has arranged for Jane to marry Duke the Red. But there is one problem, the princess does not love him; in fact, she despises him.

With the strength of a hurricane, the duke rides right past Donnie and into the castle to visit his bride-to-be.

"Be gone, messenger boy!" the guard yells, and without another word, Donnie rides off in a panic.

Inside the castle, the princess has her own troubles. The future of the kingdom rests on her shoulders. Her father is sick with old age, her mother has died of influenza, and her younger brother, Prince Peter, has been denied the throne due to his immoral ways. Jane is next in line to be queen and her future husband will be the next king, as is the tradition in Grape.

Jane yearns for the gift of true love. Every night she sits on her balcony and dreams of him, while listening to her favorite music coming faintly from the kingdom below. She dreams of a man fighting for her, battling Duke the Red and sweeping her off her feet. But every time, just as he is about to show himself, she awakens. Although she has yet to see this man, her dreams do reveal one important thing: his name.

The duke sneaks onto Jane's balcony and whispers,

"Soon we will marry, my love."

"Oh! You've startled me, you evil man! How did you get in here!"

"I have my ways. Don't be afraid, my love. Soon you will be my wife."

"Should we marry even though our love isn't true?"

"Love can grow with time, darling."

"It would take a million years for me to love a repulsive man like you," Jane replies angrily. The duke grasps Jane's arm firmly and responds,

"A queen should not speak to her king in such a manner."

Just then, Prince Peter hears the screams and enters Jane's room hurriedly.

"Is everything alright, Jane?"

"Everything is fine, Peter," says the duke, answering for Jane. "The princess was just surprised to see me. She wasn't expecting me. Isn't that right, my love?"

"I'm alright, Peter. I was caught off guard, that's all."

"My apologies, Sir Red, I didn't know you were here. I heard a shout, so I came to see what the matter was."

"No worries, my friend. Come, walk with me. I meant to thank you for taking care of that problem for me. Your potion worked miracles."

"Let's just say, when it comes to magic, my skills are always at your disposal," Peter says with a grin.

Prince Peter is the first-born son of the great King Earl Grape. During the time of the queen's illness, Peter wanted to help save his mother and took an interest in medicine. Peter became an apprentice to the doctor of kings, Dr. Winston White. Peter was devastated when the doctor's medicines failed to save her. Once his mother passed, Peter turned his back on his mentor and his craft.

Peter then took what he learned of potions and pills and used them for mischief. Dr. White had no choice but to refuse him further teachings, but before he did, Peter made copies of all the doctor's formulas and stole key materials, which Peter keeps safe in his dungeon.

Peter is so immoral that the king has sworn never to turn the kingdom over to his rule. Peter is tall and thin in stature and pale in complexion. The only shred of decency he has in him is toward his sister, who he loves dearly. He knows she's the only one that understands the struggles Peter has with his father. Peter has always dreamt of following in his father's footsteps and tries hard to convince the king that he should be the next king. But no matter how hard he tries, Peter can't seem to live up to the king's expectations.

The duke and Peter's friendship is a fickle one. Peter is intimidated by the duke. He is envious of the duke's brawn and grandeur, but most of all, he is resentful of the relationship the duke has with the king. The duke uses this to his advantage and manipulates Peter however he sees fit. Peter is under the duke's control and the two of them make a dangerous team. Dr. White believes that Peter is under a spell cast by Duke the Red's sorcerers, but his worries always seem to fall on deaf ears.

Chuckling, the duke and the prince walk away with their arms around each other's shoulders. Jane overhears them whispering but can't quite make out what is said. She loves her brother, but she knows he's up to no good. She imagines they must be devising some evil plot, which she wants no part of, so she leaves to visit with her aging father.

The princess slowly approaches the king's bedside to ask for his help with her problem.

"Father," she says softly, "are you awake?"

"Jane? Is that you?" the king struggles to reply.

"Yes, Father, it's me. The duke is here, and I still can't stand the sight of him. Please, Father, I can't marry this man; he's not right for the kingdom and I do not love him."

"Jane, you know I must do what's right for the people of Grape. Peter has lost my trust, and he cannot rule this land. I care too much for my people. General Malbec Red saved us during the civil war. I gave my word to his father; I must honor it."

"What about me, Father? Am I not of any importance to you? Do you not care about what's right for your daughter?"

"Please, Jane, you know I love you. I do not have much longer before life leaves me. Not even the magic of the great Dr. Winston White can save me now. I've done my best to find someone right for you and the kingdom. If you love me, you will marry him. It is my dying wish." Her father's words hurt, but she feels she must obey him.

"Yes, Father," the princess agrees. "I will do this, but only because my love for you is stronger than the hate I have for the duke. Just know this: the people of Grape do not respect Duke the Red - they fear him."

II

It's another warm and damp day in the kingdom, perfect for growing grapes. All the commoners are out picking the ripest of the crop, as their superiors look on. Grape is not only the name of this kingdom, but also a way of life. The grapes feed families, flavor wines, and the harvesting brings the community closer together.

Donnie starts this day with an extra spring in his step. He had an important dream last night. He had a vison of his parents, telling him to be brave and stand up for himself and to always follow his heart, no matter the cost. He dreamt of defeating the evil duke, taking the princess in his arms, and living happily ever after. Donnie has decided that today will be the day he speaks to the princess.

He quickly gets dressed and jogs confidently out the door.

"Ouch!" He cries out in pain as he carelessly stubs his toe on the door frame. Some things never change.

Donnie approaches the house of Lady Gates. As he gets closer, he sees smoke rising from her windows and chimney.

"Someone, please, call the guards! The house is on fire! Lady Gates is trapped inside! Someone please, help her!" a neighbor yells.

Without hesitation, Donnie jumps off Pinot and runs inside in search of Lady Gates. Donnie's eyes are watering, and his lungs struggle for breath. He covers his mouth with his cloak as he crouches to avoid the thick grey smoke. He hears a faint voice coming from what seems to be the kitchen. He fights his way through furniture and debris, trying to follow the voice.

"I'm here, please help!" Lady Gates pleads.

Donnie jumps up and kicks open the kitchen door. He grabs Lady Gates and leaps out the back window, just as the fire belches a massive flame in their direction.

"Thank you, thank you, please, we must save the seeds! They're in a chest in the cellar!"

Once Lady Gates is safe outside, Donnie braces himself to go back in; he must save the seeds of Grape. Donnie lunges through a window and heads downstairs.

Fighting through flames and smoke, Donnie sees the wooden chest. He tries to pry it open, but its locks are too strong. Donnie reached for his iron letter knife and snaps the lock open. He grabs the seeds and runs for the door. He makes it as far as the porch and collapses. Pinot springs into action and bites down on Donnie's collar and pulls him to safety. A crowd has formed outside the house. They all applaud as they watch Donnie and Pinot escape the blaze.

General Strum and his guards arrive on the scene along with Princess Jane. They attend to Donnie and Lady Gates as best they can. They offer them water to drink and damp rags to clean themselves. General Strum asks,

"Is everyone alright? What happened here?"

Lady Gates says, "I was preparing my morning tea when my cloth caught fire. It all happened so fast. Thankfully, a hero arrived to save me and the sacred seeds. Thank you, young man."

Donnie says,

"You're welcome, Lady Gates. I'm just happy that you're alright."

"I'm truly sorry for how I've treated you all these years, young man, bless your heart."

The general smiles and pats Donnie on the back.

"Such an act of bravery must be rewarded. Tell me your name and I will report to the king what has transpired here today."

"Donnie Drake, sir," Donnie says proudly, "Just mentioning my name to the king is reward enough, thank you. I'll be on my way now. I have plenty of messages to deliver."

Jane's eyes widen as she hears his name. Donnie mounts his horse and turns to leave. After a brief talk with some of the onlookers, Jane and four of her most trusted helpers follow the path left by Pinot's hooves. They want to learn more about their unsung hero.

The people of Grape begin to take notice that Donnie is no ordinary messenger boy. Word begins to spread that there is a hero amongst them.

Donnie is filled with joy as he continues his route. He feels the spirit of his brave parents within him. Suddenly, as he nears the castle, Donnie feels a familiar rumble. In seconds, he's thrown from Pinot and lands face first on the forest ground.

"Move boy! You move when Duke the Red rides. This is my forest. Show some respect for your future king!"

Stunned by the force of the duke's strength, Donnie carelessly mumbles back something unthinkable.

"I will not move for you, you cruel brute."

Duke the Red dismounts and walks slowly toward him.

"What did you say to me, boy?" The duke's body blocks out the sun, and the leaves rustle with an eerie sound, as if they are frightened too. Donnie dusts himself off, rises to his feet, and speaks courageously.

"I see no king here. There is no crown on your head."

"Is that so? And just who do you think you are? And what are you doing in my forest?"

"I am Donnie Drake, brave messenger of the kingdom Grape!"

Duke the Red sarcastically claps his hands. Thankfully for Donnie, the duke seems more amused than angry.

"You must be mad. Back to your physician, boy, and please, have him increase your prescription." The duke sneers as he turns to walk away.

Donnie, filled with rage, runs full speed for the duke and shoves him with all his might. Duke the Red falls with a loud clank as his heavy armor smashes into the ground. Time seems to stand still. With one swift strike, Donnie finds himself pinned to the ground with the duke looming over him, sword drawn and pressed to Donnie's cheek.

"Listen now and listen well, boy. Speak your last words, for this is the last time they will be heard."

"Wait!" calls a voice. Princess Jane and her helpers have witnessed the whole affair.

"Stop!" she cries. "I beg you! Please leave this man alone." As Donnie and Jane's eyes meet, sparks fly, and a feeling of true love fills the air. The duke seems puzzled and angered.

"But why? This man is mad! He must be banished for the safety of the kingdom."

"He is my true love."

"What? Ridiculous!" Duke the Red yells.

With the pommel of his sword, the duke delivers one last blow that knocks Donnie lifeless. Pinot tries to help but is blocked by the strength of the duke's stallion.

"Enough!" says Jane. "It comes to this, Duke. I do not love you; I never have. I dream this battle every night, and in that dream my true love's name is Donnie Drake. From all that I've seen and felt today, my heart knows this for sure." The duke takes a moment to think, then releases Donnie.

"Fine, I'll spare him, on one condition: our marriage will continue, you must marry me. I need the power; I, Duke the Red, must be king! It's that or your true love dies."

Knowing that Donnie is her only chance of true love, the princess cannot stand to lose him.

"Yes, please leave him," she pleads. "Let him live and I will marry you."

The tearful princess mounts her horse and rides towards the castle with her cruel groom-to-be, leaving behind her followers to care for Donnie, who is unconscious on the forest floor.

Luckily for Donnie, General Strum and his guards are nearby, on their way back to the castle.

The lead guard spots the crowd on the path and yells, "Halt!"

General Strum approaches.

"Is that Donnie Drake?"

"Yes, general. I believe it is."

"Wake him up and find out what happened."

"Wake up young man? Why are you lying here?" asks the guard. Donnie hesitates as his vision and wits come back to him.

"I was on my way to deliver my messages to the castle when I was knocked down. I tried to stand my ground, but he was too strong. Then, the princess arrived, they left together, that's all I remember."

"Who did this to you? Who would commit such a ruthless act?" the general asks. Donnie pauses, then says,

"Duke the Red."

"Curse that rotten man!" the general roars.

"The king shall hear of this." General Strum leaves the fallen hero in the hands of Jane's helpers as they lead Donnie back home to recover.

General Strum and the duke have always been at odds. The general knows the true story of the Red family and how they cheated and deceived to win the civil war. Also, he knows the duke has always desired his position in the army. Duke the Red believes he should General. General Strum knows he must convince the king that the kingdom cannot be left in the hands of Duke the Red.

Meanwhile, the duke and the princess arrive at the castle. Before he leaves, Duke the Red stares at Jane with evil in his eyes and reminds her of her promise.

"Remember, my dear, we marry, or your true love dies." The duke pulls on his horse's reins and rides off in a rage.

III

Donnie Drake returns home, beaten and exhausted. Not only did he receive a royal thumping, but he also believes he has lost his true love to the duke.

As he cleans himself up, he wonders what he has left to live for. If he can't have Jane, he wants nothing at all. It will be a long night of wine and song to ease the pain of his broken heart. He puts down his wine and picks up his guitar. The sounds of great sorrow echo throughout the kingdom as he plays.

Jane can hear the music from her balcony, as she stares into the night sky. She knows it's Donnie, as only true heartbreak can create those beautiful tones.

At the castle, the king and his general sit down to go over their monthly reports.

"How are you feeling, sire?" General Strum asks.

"I feel alright, general. I have the best doctor in the kingdom. He helps me get through these rough days. Now, more importantly, how is the kingdom?"

"Very well, as usual, my liege. The rock quarry and lumber mill are stocked, our water is abundant, the crops are blooming, and the army is as strong as ever. Our winemakers believe this year's Cabernet will be our finest."

"That is like music to my ears, General Strum," says the king.

"There are, however, two incidents that I must bring to your attention, my grace."

"What troubles you, old friend?"

"We seem to have a local hero among us, my liege. This morning, there was a fire at the Gates' residence. We were called by the neighbors to help save Lady Gates who was trapped inside. When we arrived, Lady Gates had been already rescued by a young man."

"And the seeds?" the king asks.

"Also saved, my lord."

"Well, that does deserve my attention. This courageous young man deserves praise and reward. Who is this valiant lad?"

"His name is Donnie Drake, the town's messenger," the general says.

"Ah yes, Donnie Drake. He came very well recommended by Lady Rose at the orphanage. She said there was something special about that young man. And the other matter?" the king asks.

"Well, it also involves Donnie Drake, my liege. Later, we found him beaten, almost to death, in the forest near the castle. When we asked what happened, we were surprised to hear that he was assaulted by none other than Duke the Red. I know

you hold the duke in high regard, but I must say I've

never trusted that man. I hear whispers that our

people fear him, my lord; the war stories are true, his

family betrayed us."

"This is troubling news," The king says. "I

trusted this man and his family. Maybe I was wrong."

Just then, the princess enters the chamber.

"Father, listen to me now. All I've ever wanted

was to make you proud." The princess begins to weep

as she tells her father how she truly feels.

Knowing this is not his place, General Strum

gets up, salutes the king, and leaves them to finish

their important discussion.

The princess continues, "If you make me

marry Duke the Red, know by morning I won't be

here, I'll be dead. I've found my true love, and his

name is Donnie Drake. He is a good man, I know it. I

wish my heart to belong to only him. The duke is evil

and will do no good ruling these lands. You must believe me."

King Earl is moved by his daughter's words. He gathers himself and speaks.

"Jane, you know I love you more than any king has ever loved a daughter before. I now can see that the duke and his family are not who I believed them to be. If it is Donnie Drake you want, then consider it done."

The king and princess share a loving embrace, and Princess Jane leaves her father's chamber with a weight lifted off her shoulders.

After hearing what has transpired from both the general and his daughter, the king's view of Duke the Red has changed. He has always heard how the Red family used sorcery and torture to win the war in order to gain the king's favor, but he refused to believe it.

He must find a way to break up the marriage and regain his daughter's trust. The duke will not take this news lightly, nor will his family. The king knows of no man who is any match for the duke's strength. He must defeat him by some other means. The king needs someone who is close to him. He knows of only one man who can help him now. The king turns to his royal guard and says,

"Guard, bring me my son. Bring Prince Peter forth."

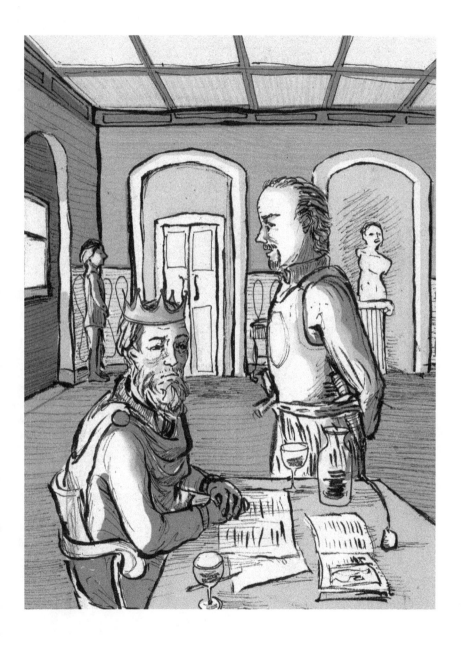

IV

With morning arriving and the wedding day looming, Peter and the king have devised a masterful plan. The only thing left for King Earl and Prince Peter to do is to visit Donnie Drake. With a little medical magic from Dr. Winston White, the king uses all the power he has left for his last journey. He pushes himself off his bed and prepares for his voyage.

As they reach Cherry Street, they hear the melodies of a broken man. Prince Peter notices Donnie's door is open. He and the king slowly push open the creaking wooden door and enter without notice.

"Donnie Drake?" Peter calls.

"There's no man with that name here. That man has died of a broken heart."

"That is a shame. The king is here and would love to make his acquaintance."

Donnie turns to see the king, only to trip and fall carelessly in the process.

"What? The king? Here?" One look at the ruler of Grape and Donnie straightens up and salutes. "My liege."

The king speaks.

"If my dear Jane has her way, soon people will be bowing to you."

"That would be a dream, my liege. Although, it would seem the princess has had a change of heart." Donnie's emotions quickly change. "I was in battle with Duke the Red when she came to my rescue. I was knocked out and when I came to, they were gone. Now, I hear plans of a wedding."

"Jane has only agreed to marry the duke in order to save your life. It was either accept his terms, or you would be killed. I think she made the correct decision, don't you?" Jane's father's kind eyes fall on Donnie. Donnie answers with a smile.

"Yes, my liege."

"I've heard what you've done. You are a hero, you are brave; you stood up to Duke the Red, despite his power. You saved Lady Gates and our sacred seeds. But most importantly, my daughter dreams of you and knows that you are her one true love. I see a lot of my dear wife in you. Oh, how I miss my sweet Mary, I wish she were here to help us." Donnie is overjoyed at the king's words.

"Thank you, my king. You have touched me with your kind words. I share the same feelings for Jane. But what do we do about the duke?"

"Now hear this. I love my daughter and my kingdom, and I will do everything in my power to please them both. After speaking with Jane, Prince

Peter and I have come up with a plan to stop the

wedding. Prince Peter will explain."

"I've created an extraordinary potion," Peter

says, "Once ingested, the potion will force the duke to

obey my every word. Once he's under my control, I

will command him to ride off and never return."

"But how will you make him drink?" Donnie

asks. Peter answers with a grin,

"I will simply ask, my dear Donnie. After all, it

is his wedding day. He will have no choice but to

accept. Once the duke is gone, the real wedding will

begin, the marriage of Jane Grape and Donnie

Drake." Donnie agrees.

Peter grabs the bottle of wine Donnie has been

drinking from, wipes off three glasses from his

cabinet, pours three drinks, and proposes a toast.

"So, it is done. The king and I will return to

the castle to inform Jane of the good news. Let us

drink for good luck, yes? I promise there are no potions in these cups." They all share a good laugh and drink every drop.

As night arrives, Peter and the king return to the castle feeling closer to each other than ever before. They walk elegantly though the grand corridor, which is dimly lit by the iron scones burning gently on the stone walls. As they approach the king's chambers, Peter speaks.

"Father, let me help you into bed."

"Thank you, Peter. You know, it feels great to finally do something together as a family. I'm proud of you, my son. Can you fetch me my medication?"

"Yes, father."

Peter pauses as he considers what he is about to do. He hasn't heard a compliment from his father since he was a young boy. But it's not enough to stop Peter from getting what he feels he rightly deserves.

He reaches into his pocket and switches Dr. White's prescribed pills with his own and carefully places them in his father's hands.

"Here you go, Father. Sleep tight," Peter says as he kisses his father's forehead.

V

The day of the wedding has arrived. The new
bride gets ready in her room with her handmaidens.
She looks stunning in her light blue wedding dress,
royal jewelry, and glistening in anticipation of her
marriage. One of her maidens says,

"You look beautiful, Jane. You seem so happy.
I thought you despised the duke?"

"Thank you, Margaret. For the first time in my
life I am truly happy. Let's just say the duke is a
different person to me now," Jane says. The prince
enters the room with a sad look on his face.

"Jane, darling, you look absolutely breathtaking."

"Thank you, brother. What's wrong?"

"Jane, I have some sad news. Our father has passed." They share a long and tearful embrace, mourning the loss of their father.

"I'm sorry, Jane. Dr. White woke me and told me that this was Father's last morning. With his final breath, Father told me that he loves you and will always be with you. Jane, you knew his health was poor. Let's go on and be strong for our father."

"When did this happen? Why didn't you send for me?"

"I wanted to, but Father insisted. He didn't want you to witness him at his weakest hour. He wanted you to remember him as a strong man who loved you very much. He wanted you to be happy during this special moment in your life."

"I'll be strong. I will dedicate this day to him, the greatest king Grape has ever known," Jane says with tears in her eyes. After one last embrace, Prince Peter heads straight to his underground lair.

Peter works frantically, mixing and pouring, whipping up his concoction. He needs to make it just right to slay a giant like Duke the Red. There is no potion made, poison is on the menu.

"Your grace, Duke the Red has arrived." A guard interrupts.

A smile comes over the prince's face. He quickly hides his tools.

"Ah, yes, please send him down." Peter prepares the table with two glasses of wine and carefully slips the mixture into the duke's glass.

"Duke, please, come down and drink with me on this historic day."

"Of course, Peter. I just heard the good news. Is the king dead? Did our plan work?"

"Yes, the king has passed, with a little help from my pills of course. The tough part was convincing Dr. White that the death was natural; thankfully, the doctor's magic has limits." They raise their glasses as Peter begins his toast.

"Now, with my father gone, cheers to my brother and the new ruler of the Kingdom Grape."

"Hear, hear, Peter! I won't forget what you have done for me. Together we will rule this kingdom, just as we've planned."

Little does the duke know, Prince Peter has no intention of sharing the kingdom with anyone. The duke raises his glass and drinks with the prince. Before the glass hits the table, the duke can taste the poison in his throat. He lunges at Peter. But it is too late. Duke the Red is dead.

The prince takes a moment to admire his work. But he knows his work is not done. He struggles with what he must do next. He paces back and forth, trying desperately to figure out another way. Regrettably, He knows it's the only way he can get the throne that he so desires.

He straightens up, dusts himself off, locks the door behind him, and walks up the stairs. He has an important wedding to attend.

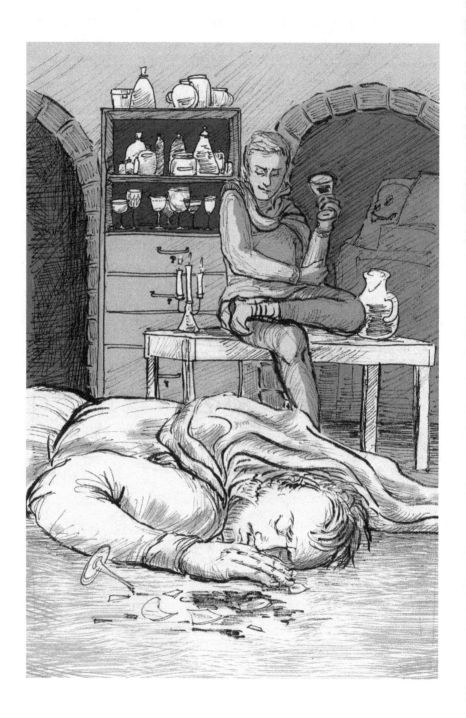

VI

The castle is alive with the sights and sounds of a glorious royal wedding. The grounds have been decorated by the finest designers, and only the most talented flutists have been selected to perform.

All the people of Grape are in attendance to witness this historic moment. They all march together down to the courtyard where the ceremony is to take place. The people are astonished to see Donnie Drake standing as the groom, waiting for his bride to be. The people are relieved as whispers of the duke's demise are heard, and word begins to spread that Donnie Drake will be the new king.

The priest has arrived, and everyone is in place for the proceedings to begin. The brass horns play the traditional wedding march as the bride is led down the aisle by her proud brother.

Jane looks breathtaking in her long flowing gown with a perfect blue orchid pinned in her hair. All eyes are on the beautiful bride, while she looks down the aisle at her true love.

The priest says, "Dearly beloved, we are gathered here today to celebrate the marriage of Donnie Drake and Jane Grape." The priest proudly conducts his ceremony as a great cheer comes from the crowd.

As the ceremony comes to an end, the priest turns to introduce the new king.

"Now, our new king, Donnie Drake, has prepared some words." After a loud roar from the people, Donnie speaks, smiling nervously.

"Thank you, Father Bobal. Jane, from the moment I laid eyes on you I knew you were my true love. I would watch you and admire how you would comfort everyone on your daily rides. You treated everyone as equal. I thought such a beautiful and wonderful person like you would never think to marry a common messenger boy like me, but I was wrong. The gods have given us this great gift of true love. I will love you and support you till the day I die."

Donnie leans over and kisses his wife for the first time. He then addresses his people, speaking with pride and elegance.

"To the people of Grape, I will do my very best to be a great king to the land that I love. I will follow in the footsteps of the greatest king we were ever blessed with, King Earl Grape. Together, we will prosper and live in peace."

A deafening cheer comes from the thousands of onlookers adoring their new ruler.

The prince says,

"If I could, I would also like to share a few words."

"Of course, brother," says Jane. "we would be honored."

"First, to my new king and queen, I wish you love, luck, and a long and healthy life together. Secondly, to everyone in attendance, I know my actions over the years have been dire and I've treated you unfairly. I am deeply sorry for all my wrongdoing. Last, and most important, to my father, please watch over us and protect us so we may live in everlasting harmony." Peter weeps as he speaks. His words touch everyone in attendance. Jane turns to her brother.

"Thank you, Peter. I have always been on your side and will always love you. I am forever grateful for what you've done for me and for Donnie."

Peter begins to sweat as he feels the pressure of the moment. He hugs Jane.

"I propose a toast. To the new king and queen, and to the entire kingdom; let us live in peace, good health and prosperity!"

Blinded by this special moment on this special day, Jane and Donnie carelessly drink every drop of Peter's offering.

An eerie silence comes over the crowd of thousands as Jane and Donnie stumble and collapse from the poison in their drinks. Peter's demeaner quickly changes from love to evil.

"Did you really think that I would let you have the kingdom that our father unfairly denied me? Peter continues and shouts. "Ladies and gentlemen, Donnie and Jane are no longer. I, Peter Grape, am your new king!"

The silence continues as King Peter retreats to the castle to celebrate his victory. The royal army follows as they must obey their sacred oath to protect the king.

The rest of the town hurries to the aid of their fallen heroes. They crowd around the duo, desperate to find any signs of life. But it's too late; Donnie and Jane have passed.

Suddenly, a man appears in the distance, covered head to toe in a long white cloak and carrying a large leather satchel. The people of Grape part to allow the man a clear path. All is quiet except the whispering of his name. "It's the doctor of kings, Dr. Winston White."

As the doctor approaches the fallen couple, he opens his satchel and searches for what he needs.

"Can you save them, doctor?" someone shouts from the crowd.

"That depends," Dr. White replies. "I cannot cure those who have died of natural causes, which is the will of the gods. Donnie and Jane clearly have not died naturally. Also, my magic only works for those who are good. There are two types of people in this world, those who spread love and joy, and those who spread evil and hate. My magic is reserved for the noble. I know Jane very well. I am proud of the good in her heart. Donnie is a brave and heroic man respected by the people of Grape. Therefore, I indeed have the cure."

Dr. White grabs a jug from his satchel, removes the top, and out flies the antidote, a never-ending stream of white butterflies from ancient Grape. These butterflies are known to hold the power of life. They haven't been seen in centuries. They hover over Jane and Donnie as if to first approve their worthiness, then what happens next is nothing short of amazing. They fly in sequence through the air with their wings dancing in perfect rhythm. A blinding light appears as they release the magic elements which hold the cure for the fallen couple.

Donnie and Jane slowly open their eyes to see the

people of Grape rejoicing.

"Thank you, doctor. You have given us the gift

of life. How can we possibly repay you?" asks Jane.

"Please, I don't deserve reward. I feel

responsible for giving Peter the knowledge to produce

such destruction. I should have cured him from his

curse long ago. It is I who will be forever in debt."

"None of this is your fault. We should have

listened when you told us of Peter's struggles. We will

do everything in our power to rid Grape of my

brother's torment."

"How can we possibly defeat a man of such

treachery?" a woman asks. Feeling his people's fear,

Donnie addresses them.

"Today we have the chance to take back this

great land we love. It needs you more now than ever

before. We cannot defeat this evil alone, but I am

sure together we will prevail." A calm falls over the crowd as Donnie continues. "Now I ask you, what makes this kingdom so great? What is it that defines us? What is it that we do best?"

A hush comes over the crowd as they think of the solution to this important riddle. Donnie looks at Jane and can see that she has the answer. She says,

"It's simple. It's in our name, the Kingdom of Grape! We can use our grapes!" The crowd seems puzzled. A man from the crowd says,

"But how can a harmless grape defeat a man of pure evil?" Jane replies,

"We defeat him at his own game. Dr. White, you say my brother can be cured, then let us cure him. You create the potion and we will take care of the rest. My brother is ill, and no matter what he's done, he's still my brother and I love him. I know somewhere inside him there's a good man, he just needs our help to bring it out."

"There is one problem Jane. After I denied your brother my teachings, he stole the materials I need to create this potion. I hear he keeps them in his dungeon," Dr. White says.

Donnie speaks with courage, "I will get what you need, doctor."

Jane reaches for Donnie's arm, "You'll need my help."

VII

Night comes quickly as a thick fog begins to creep over the hills as the pivotal moment arrives. Everyone in the kingdom has a vital role to play. They must release the kingdom from the grip of evil and return it to the people of Grape.

Donnie and Jane slowly make their way to the front gates of the castle to begin their plan. Donnie turns to Jane.

"There are guards everywhere. How can we possibly get in?"

Jane smiles and says,

"I've been sneaking in and out of this castle for years, even princesses need to have some fun."

They sneak around to the castle's stables. Jane motions to Donnie.

"Follow me."

She carefully moves a bale of hay which is propped up against a wall to reveal a tunnel. Donnie smiles.

"You are a sneaky girl."

They quickly ignite their torches and make their way into the castle. They scurry through the dark tunnel which leads to Jane's bedroom. Jane reaches under her bed and pulls out her royal sword.

"Even princesses must defend themselves."

"You're just full of surprises, aren't you?" says Donnie.

Donnie opens Jane's door and clutches his iron letter knife as they make their way down a corridor which leads to the dungeon stairwell. As they approach the stairwell, they notice two guards at their posts.

"What do we do now?" Jane asks.

"There's only one thing we can do. We fight for the kingdom."

They gather up all their courage and begin to walk toward the stairwell. Suddenly, General Strum appears behind the two guards. He grabs both their helmets and smashes them together. The guards drop to the ground with a loud thump.

"I knew you two would come. Hurry, you don't have much time. Peter is asleep."

Donnie looks him in the eyes and says,

"Thank you."

Meanwhile, Peter tosses and turns in his bed; he's having trouble getting to sleep. He is struggling with what he's done. He hears a commotion coming from the stairwell. Half asleep and not sure if he's just hearing things, he lights his torch and goes down to investigate. As he opens the door to his dungeon, he can't believe his eyes - its Donnie and Jane.

"No! It can't be! You're dead!" Peter screams and runs back to his chamber, certain he's just seen ghosts. He jumps into bed and repeats, "It's just a dream. It's just a dream..."

Donnie and Jane quickly ransack through all of Peter's chests and cabinets trying to find the materials Dr. White listed. Peter turns over a leather-bound book with the right inscriptions and stuffs it under his belt.

"Jane I've got the formulas, have you found the chemicals?"

"I see them, but they are all unlabeled."

Donnie quickly skims through Peter's book and finds a legend. He compares it with Winston's list and describes to Jane what they need.

"Yes! I have it."

They quickly secure their findings and head back to deliver them to Dr. White.

Morning comes and Peter marches directly to his general.

"General Strum, last night, I had a vision of my sister and Donnie Drake. Please tell me I was just imagining things?"

"You must have been, my liege. We were all on high alert. A few of our men have been exiled, but nothing was out of the ordinary. I can assure you, Donnie and Jane are no longer with us."

"Yes. Yes, of course. Forget I mentioned it. I must have been dreaming. You know what they say, 'heavy lies the crown'."

Convinced it was all a bad dream, Peter begins to cherish his first day as king. He summons jesters for entertainment and commands his servants to send for wine and a feast.

As he finishes his last bite, Peter hears a knock on the castle gates. A guard looks through the portcullis and says,

"It's the people of Grape, my lord; it seems they've come bearing gifts. Shall I let them enter?"

"I knew they would come around to praise me. Let my people in, so they can honor their new king."

The people of Grape enter the castle and put on a show, all dressed in costume and singing and dancing. They all play their parts perfectly.

Peter speaks. "My people, I am relieved that you have come to accept me as your new ruler. We will be strong, bold, and fierce. We will form a great army to conquer the lands beyond our own. People will fear us!"

A masked man dressed in full costume walks up to the king's throne with a gift. Guards rush to intercept, but the king waves them off and allows the man to draw near.

The man speaks. "My liege, to show our devotion to you, we have picked the finest grapes in the kingdom and offer them to you as a gift."

The man's voice sounds familiar to the new king, but he thinks nothing of it. He's too distracted by the love he's feeling from his people. He accepts the gift.

"I couldn't think of a better dessert to end my first feast."

Just as Peter swallows the last of his grapes, the man removes his mask to reveal himself. Peter's eyes open wide as he sees Donnie's face. Peter looks at the crowd in horror as he falls to the ground, paralyzed and in shock.

A feeling of warmth comes over him as Dr. White's potion takes over. He begins to feel different, as if a weight has been lifted from his shoulders and fog has been removed from his thoughts. The familiar feeling of good starts to fill his body. Peter has finally been cured of his demons.

"I'm cured! I'm cured! Thank you. Thank you. You have given me my life back. I can once again feel joy. I'm sorry for all I've done. As long as I am a part of this family, and this glorious kingdom, that is all the power I need. I am honored to hand you this." Peter hands Donnie the crown that he so rightly deserves.

A true cheer comes from the crowd as the people begin to rejoice. Dr. White and General Strum celebrate together, while Lady Gates and Lady Rose dance with excitement. Pinot finds Jane and gracefully lowers his head as she mounts and trots proudly towards Donnie. Jane dismounts, gives Pinot a big hug, removes her mask, and runs up to the throne to join Donnie in their rightful place, as king and queen of the Kingdom of Grape.

Donnie and Jane would go on to lead the kingdom through many years of peace and prosperity. They would have children of their own: two daughters, Princess Nelleah and Princess Alyssa.

Prince Peter would later rejoin Dr. Winston White and once again practice medicine. Eventually, after Dr. White's retirement, Peter would become Dr. Grape and follow admirably in his mentor's footsteps.

As the good in Peter continues to grow, so too do the great vines of the Kingdom of Grape.

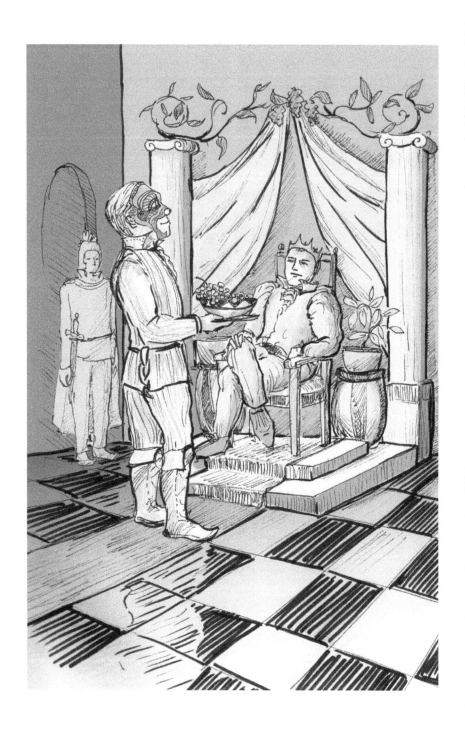

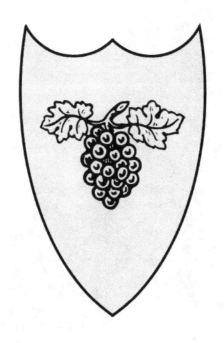

ABOUT THE AUTHOR

Raimo Strangis is a fiction writer from Toronto,
Ontario, Canada. As well as writing, Raimo is a
professional Chef and accomplished Songwriter.

CPSIA information can be obtained
at www.ICGtesting.com
Printed in the USA
LVHW110134231122
733823LV00023B/340